W9-BDU-312

Honest Ashley

Virginia Kroll

illustrated by **Nancy Cote**

Albert Whitman & Company, Morton Grove, Illinois

With love to Alyssa Ceriani, Mia Ceriani, Molly Kabza,
and especially Ashley Kabza.—V.K.

To Mike, Kate, Missy, and John—the best family in the whole world.
Love always.—N.C.

The Way I Act Books:

Forgiving a Friend · *Jason Takes Responsibility* · *Honest Ashley* · *Ryan Respects*

The Way I Feel Books:

When I Care about Others · *When I Feel Angry*

When I Feel Good about Myself · *When I Feel Jealous*

When I Feel Sad · *When I Feel Scared* · *When I Miss You*

Library of Congress Cataloging-in-Publication Data

Kroll, Virginia L.
Honest Ashley / by Virginia Kroll ; illustrated by Nancy Cote.
p. cm. — (The way I act)
Summary: When Ashley postpones a homework assignment until the last minute, she is tempted
to pass off an old paper of her brother's as her own.
ISBN 13: 978-0-8075-3371-0 (hardcover)
ISBN 10: 0-8075-3371-8 (hardcover)
[1. Honesty—Fiction. 2. Homework—Fiction.] I. Cote, Nancy, ill. II. Title. III. Series.
PZ7.K9227Hon 2006 [E]—dc22 2005024864

Text copyright © 2006 by Virginia Kroll.
Illustrations copyright © 2006 by Nancy Cote.
Published in 2006 by Albert Whitman & Company,
6340 Oakton Street, Morton Grove, Illinois 60053-2723.
Published simultaneously in Canada by Fitzhenry & Whiteside, Markham, Ontario.
Printed in the United States.
10 9 8 7 6 5 4 3 2 1

The design is by Carol Gildar.

For more information about Albert Whitman & Company, please visit our web site at www.albertwhitman.com.

On Monday after school,
Ashley told Mom, "Mrs. Marshall said our writing project
for Friday is to tell about something that happened in the
neighborhood. I don't know what I'll write about."

"I'm sure you'll have a great idea before Friday," Mom said.
Ashley wasn't worried. She had lots of time.

But by the time Ashley had helped with the dinner dishes, she still hadn't thought of an idea. "Oh, well, I'll think about it tomorrow," she said and went next door to her cousin Carly's. They had fun painting rocks.

On Tuesday, Ashley walked Mr. Garvey's pug, Pippin, and watched too much TV.

On Wednesday, Ashley went with Dad to her big brother Steven's basketball game. Then they all got ice cream.

On Thursday, Ashley's friend Kelly stayed over till after eight. Just before Kelly's mother picked her up, Ashley remembered. "Oh, no! I forgot all about my writing assignment!"

"Me, too," said Kelly. "But I just asked my sister, Laura, to write it while I was here. She owes me a favor, anyway."

"Isn't that cheating, Kelly?" Ashley whispered, hoping their mothers weren't listening. "I mean, isn't that like stealing someone else's work?"

"So what?" said Kelly. "Laura loves to write. Plus she writes a lot better than I do, so I'll get a good grade for sure."

Ashley didn't know what to say.

After Kelly had gone, Ashley quickly brushed her teeth and put on her pajamas. She got out her composition notebook and pencil. Mom and Dad came in to say goodnight.

"What are you doing?" Mom asked.

"My writing project," Ashley answered. "I forgot all about it, and it's due tomorrow."

"Too bad," said Dad, taking Ashley's notebook and pencil and setting them on her desk. "Lights out. It's too late for homework."

Ashley pouted. Her parents kissed her and tucked her in. Mom said, "Maybe you can get up a little early and do it in the morning."

"Or maybe not," Ashley muttered to her hippo, Hugo, when her parents had left the room. "Maybe Kelly had the right idea. I should've asked Steven."

But Ashley knew that Steven wouldn't help her cheat even if he owed her fifty favors.

She snuggled down and hugged Hugo. A sudden idea made her bolt right back up. *Mom keeps all our special papers in the trunk in the guest room!*

Ashley opened her door. She could hear the TV
and Mom, Dad, and Steven talking. She crept down the
hall and into the guest room.

The trunk's latch opened with a soft click. Up went the lid. It didn't take Ashley long to find what she was looking for: a large brown envelope marked **Steven—Third Grade.**

Her heart pounded as she shut the trunk. She clasped the envelope and hurried back to bed.

Ashley leafed through the papers. There it was: "About My Neighbor," by Steven Arida. Steven had been in Mrs. Marshall's class four years ago. *She'll never remember,* Ashley thought.

By the light of the hallway, Ashley started copying Steven's story as fast as she could. It was about his babysitter, Linda.

By accident, Mom had given Linda too much money because two brand-new ten-dollar bills had been stuck together. Linda had come back and returned one that very night. Mom said, "Why, Linda, I never would have known the difference."

Linda replied, "But I did. It wouldn't have been honest to keep it."

Steven had made Linda sound like a hero.

When Ashley came to the word *honest*, she got a knot in her stomach. She knew why. "This just won't work, Hugo," she said. "I can't cheat."

Ashley slid Steven's story into
the envelope. Then she tiptoed to the
trunk and put the story back. She got
to her room again just as she heard
the TV go off.

The next morning, Ashley woke up early on her own.
She quickly wrote about the time that Mr. McLimans went
to grab the morning paper and got locked out of his house.
He had to knock and ask to use the phone to call his wife.
He was fresh from the shower, and his dog, Daisy, kept
tugging at his towel!

It had been pretty funny.

At school, after Ashley and her classmates had shared their stories, Mrs. Marshall said, "I've kept copies of three superb examples written by former students." She read each one out loud. The second story was Steven's!

Ashley gulped, then took a long, deep sigh of relief.
She looked over at Kelly, but Kelly was staring at her desk.
Was she thinking about cheating?

On Ashley's composition, Mrs. Marshall had written, "This is good, but it could be excellent, Ashley. Next time, don't rush it."

That night, Ashley showed Hugo her grade.
"I got a plain old B," she said.

But it was an honest *B*, because
it belonged only to her.